MW00932181

FUNNY JOKES

FOR

YEAR OLD KIDS

HUNDREDS OF HILARIOUS JOKES INSIDE!

JIMMY JONES

Hundreds of really funny, hilarious jokes that will have the kids in fits of laughter in no time!

They're all in here - the funniest
- Jokes
- Riddles
- Tongue Twisters
- Knock Knock Jokes

for 5 year old kids!

Funny kids love funny jokes and this brand new collection of original and classic jokes promises hours of fun for the whole family!

Books by Jimmy Jones

Funny Jokes For Funny Kids
Knock Knock Jokes For Funny Kids

Funny Jokes For Kids Series
All Ages 5 -12!

To see all the latest books by
Jimmy Jones just go to
kidsjokebooks.com

Copyright © 2018. All rights reserved. No part of this publication may be reproduced, distributed or transmitted in any form or by any means, including photocopying or other mechanical or electronic methods without the written permission of the publisher, except in the case of non-commercial uses permitted by copyright law.

Contents

Funny Jokes!

Why do mice have a bath?
To feel squeaky clean!

Why don't eggs tell jokes?
They might crack up laughing!

How did the clam call her friend?
On her shell phone!

Where do chickens go for a laugh?
The funny farm!

Where did the dog park his car?
The Barking Lot!

What did the fairy use to clean her teeth?
Fairy Floss!

What did one egg say to the other egg?
Let's get cracking!

Why did the polar bear have a fur coat?
He lost his sweater!

Why didn't the moon finish its dinner?
It was full!

What do crabs do on their birthday?
They shell-abrate!

What do you get if you dive into the Red Sea?
Wet!

Where do fish keep their money?
In the river bank!

What do you call a girl who likes to cook outside?

Barbie!

Why did the cat swim?

She was a platy-puss!

Why did the berry call 911?

She was in a jam!

Why did the girl take her ruler to bed?
To see how long she slept!

Why do wasps get so much done in a day?
They are busy bees!

What do puppies eat at the movies?
Pupcorn!

Why did the boy run around his bed?
To catch up on his sleep!

How do koalas fight?
With their bear hands!

How can you cut a wave in half?
With a sea saw!

What do dancers like to drink?
Tap water!

Why did the lamb go to the mall?
To go to the baarber shop!

Who plays music on your head?
The headband!

What shoes do mice wear?
Squeakers!

Why are fish really clever?
They live in schools!

Why did the almond jump up and down?
It was going nuts!

How can you tell when a train is eating its lunch?

It goes choo-choo!

Why did the frog say Mooooo?

He was learning to speak cow!

Why should you never tell a joke while standing on ice?

It might crack up!

Why was the wall cold?
He needed another coat of paint!

What do you call a witch at the beach?
A sandwitch!

Why did the cow wear a bell?
Her horn didn't work!

Why did the photo go to jail?
It was framed!

What is the quietest dog in the world?
A hush puppy!

How did the artist keep clean?
He drew a bath!

Why did the egg hide?
It was a little chicken!

Why did the boy stand on a cow?
To be a cowboy!

What do frogs eat on really hot days?
Hop-sicles!

Why are baby cows so cute?
They are adora-bull!

What did the mommy chicken call her baby?
Egg!

What did the cat say when it fell over?
Me-ow!

What do cats put in their drinks?
Mice Cubes!

How did the girl get stung at school?
There was a spelling bee!

When is it bad luck if a black cat follows you?
When you are a grey mouse!

What do you call a bear with no teeth?
A gummy bear!

Why did the unicorn cross the road?
The chicken was sick!

Why did the cat sit on the chair?
It was PURRR-ple!

What is a frog's favorite game?
Hop scotch!

Why did the dog sit next to the tree?
She liked its bark!

Where can you make a banana split?
Sundae school!

What do fish like to watch on TV?
Whale of Fortune!

What is a good gift for a baby ghost?
Boootees!

Why was the cat scared of the tree?
Because of its bark!

Where do whales get fast food?
The dive through!

How do bees get smarter?
They have a spelling bee!

What do you call a boy on your doorstep?
Matt!

Which bird steals soap from the bathtub?
The robber duck!

Why was the broom late for school?
She overswept!

What is the worst type of jam?
A traffic jam!

What did the taxi driver say to the frog?
Hop in!

What did the snowman eat for breakfast?
Snowflakes!

How do birds learn to fly for the very first time?
They wing it!

What do you call a girl with a frog on her head?

Lily!

What do cats eat for desert?

Mice cream!

Why was the lamp sad at the beach?

He forgot to bring his shades!

Why do birds fly north in spring?
It's too far to walk!

What kind of dog did the ghost have?
A boodle!

Why did the girl love her cat?
She was purr-fect!

What shoes do ghosts wear on a cold day?
Booooooots!

Why is the ocean always so clean?
Mermaids!

What kind of tie does a boy pig wear?
A pigsty!

What kind of cat loves water?
An octopuss!

What do you use to wrap a cloud?
A rainbow!

What do you call your dad when he is covered in snow?
Pop-sicle!

How does a bee get to work?
He waits at the buzz stop!

What did the baby corn ask his mother?
Where is pop corn?

What is the best lunch in the desert?
A sandwich!

What car do insects drive?
A beetle!

What is Santa's dog called?
Santa Paws!

What fruit do horses love?
Straw-berries!

What do acrobats do on hot days?
Summer saults!

What time do ducks wake up?
The quack of dawn!

What do ghosts like for dinner?
Gumboo!

What game to mice play?
Hide and squeak!

Why did the snowman wear a bow tie?
To go to the snowball!

What did the fish take when she was sick?
Vitamin sea!

Funny Knock Knock Jokes!

Knock knock.

Who's there?

Hayden.

Hayden who?

Hayden seek is fun! Let's play!

Knock knock.

Who's there?

Hamish.

Hamish who?

Hamish you so much when I don't see you!

Knock knock.

Who's there?

Eddy.

Eddy who?

Eddy body home, I ran out of food!

Knock knock.

Who's there?

Alaska.

Alaska who?

Alaska when I see her!

Knock knock.

Who's there?

Candice.

Candice who?

Candice door open any faster if I push it?

Knock knock.

Who's there?

Adam.

Adam who?

If you Adam up I'll pay half the bill!

Knock knock.

Who's there?

Gopher.

Gopher who?

Gopher help quick! I think I broke my leg! Owwww!!

Knock knock.

Who's there?

Funnel.

Funnel who?

Funnel start in just a minute! Woohoo!

Knock knock.

Who's there?

Lefty.

Lefty who?

Lefty key at home so I had to knock!

Knock knock.

Who's there?

Quacker.

Quacker who?

Quacker another funny joke!

I love them!

Knock knock.

Who's there?

Icy.

Icy who?

Icy you had a haircut. It looks great!

Knock knock.

Who's there?

Adair.

Adair who?

Adair when I was younger but now I'm bald!

Knock knock.

Who's there?

Russian.

Russian who?

I'm Russian to get to school! Let's go!

Knock knock.

Who's there?

Jim.

Jim who?

Jim mind if I stay for a while? I got locked out of my own house!

Knock knock.

Who's there?

Figs.

Figs who?

Please figs your step.

I nearly tripped!

Knock knock.

Who's there?

Pop.

Pop who?

Pop on over to my place! We're

having ice cream!

Knock knock.

Who's there?

Matthew.

Matthew who?

Matthew lace has come undone!

Help!

Knock knock.

Who's there?

Razor.

Razor who?

Razor hands! This is a stick up!

Knock knock.

Who's there?

Philip.

Philip who?

Philip up the pool so we can have a swim! It's so hot!

Knock knock.

Who's there?

Harry.

Harry who?

Harry up! We have to go! Quick!

Knock knock.

Who's there?

Pasta.

Pasta who?

Pasta salt and pepper please!

Knock knock.

Who's there?

Yah.

Yah who?

Yahoo! Ride 'em cowboy!

Knock knock.

Who's there?

Barbie.

Barbie who?

Barbie Q for dinner! Yummy!

Knock knock.

Who's there?

Fanny.

Fanny who?

Fanny body knocks just pretend you're not home!

Knock knock.

Who's there?

Beef.

Beef who?

Beef-ore I freeze please open this door!

Knock knock.

Who's there?

Cattle.

Cattle who?

Cattle purr if you pat it!

Knock knock.

Who's there?

Doris.

Doris who?

Doris a bit squeaky! I think you need to oil it!

Knock knock.

Who's there?

Sister.

Sister who?

Sister right place for the party tonight?

Knock knock.

Who's there?

Jaws.

Jaws who?

Jaws truly! Surprise!

Knock knock.

Who's there?

Annie.

Annie who?

Annie idea when this rain will stop?

I'm getting wet!

Knock knock.

Who's there?

Amos.

Amos who?

Amos say you look great in that suit.

Where did you get it?

Knock knock.

Who's there?

Wilfred.

Wilfred who?

Wilfred be able to come out to play?

Knock knock.

Who's there?

Avenue.

Avenue who?

Avenue fixed the doorbell yet? It's still broken!

Knock knock.

Who's there?

Frank.

Frank who?

Frank you very much for finally opening this door.

Knock knock.

Who's there?

Chicken.

Chicken who?

Better chicken the oven! Something is burning!

Knock knock.

Who's there?

Ida.

Ida who?

Ida rather be inside than out here in the rain!

Knock knock.

Who's there?

Harmony.

Harmony who?

Harmony times do I have to knock?

Knock knock.

Who's there?

Lucy.

Lucy who?

Lucy lastic and your pants fall down!

Knock knock.

Who's there?

Nobel.

Nobel who?

Nobel so I have to knock knock!

Knock knock.

Who's there?

Mayan.

Mayan who?

A Mayan the way? Should I move?

Knock knock.

Who's there?

Olive.

Olive who?

Olive here but I forgot my key!

Knock knock.

Who's there?

Cook.

Cook who?

Are you a cuckoo clock?

Knock knock.

Who's there?

Ears.

Ears who?

Ears another funny joke!

Knock knock.

Who's there?

Van.

Van who?

Van are you going to let me in?

I'm hungry!

Knock knock.

Who's there?

Kenya.

Kenya who?

Kenya keep the noise down?

I'm trying to sleep!

Knock knock.

Who's there?

Foster.

Foster who?

Foster than a speeding bullet!

Knock knock.

Who's there?

Adore.

Adore who?

Adore is between us. Open it now!

Knock knock.

Who's there?

Jester.

Jester who?

Jester minute!

Where's your doorbell?

Knock knock.

Who's there?

Utah.

Utah who?

Utah one who asked me over!

Remember?

Knock knock.

Who's there?

Pasture.

Pasture who?

It's way pasture bedtime! Go to bed!

Knock knock.

Who's there?

Alpaca.

Alpaca who?

Alpaca the suitcase, you pack a the trunk!

Knock knock.

Who's there?

Boo.

Boo who?

Don't cry so much, it's only a joke!

Knock knock.

Who's there?

Ben.

Ben who?

Ben meaning to call in for ages!

How have you been?

Knock knock.

Who's there?

Dishes.

Dishes who?

Dishes the police! Open up!

Knock knock.

Who's there?

Gopher.

Gopher who?

Gopher help quick! My foot is stuck!

Knock knock.

Who's there?

Water.

Water who?

Water beautiful day! I love the sun!

Knock knock.

Who's there?

Witches.

Witches who?

Witches the fastest way to my house from here?

Knock knock.

Who's there?

Maya.

Maya who?

Maya come in? It's an emergency!

Knock knock.

Who's there?

Arthur.

Arthur who?

Arthur any leftovers from lunch?

I'm really hungry!

Knock knock.

Who's there?

Tank.

Tank who?

Tank goodness you finally answered

the door!

Funny Riddles!

What kind of button won't undo?
A belly button!

If a boomerang doesn't come back, what is it?
A stick!

Why did the banana go to hospital?
He wasn't peeling very well!

What sport do horses love?
Stable tennis!

What is the biggest ant?
An eleph-ant!

What is small, round, white, lives in a jar and laughs?
A tickled onion!

What sort of music do frogs listen to?
Hip Hop!

Why did the bird go to hospital?
To get some tweetment!

Why was 6 really scared of 7?
7, 8, 9!(Seven ate nine!)

What can you serve but never eat?
A tennis ball!

Why is the ocean always so clean?
Mermaids!

What do you call two banana peels?
Slippers!

What do you call a fly that has lost its wings?
A walk!

What sound does a chicken's phone make?
Wing Wing!

What has a bottom at the top?
Your legs!

How can you count lots of cows?
Use a cowculator!

No matter how many times you try, which word is always spelt wrong?
Wrong!

Why did the golfer go to the dentist?
She had a hole in one!

Why couldn't the aliens get a park on the moon?
It was full!

What side of a bird has the most feathers?
The outside!

Why do tigers eat raw meat?
They never learned to cook!

Which bet has never been won?
The alphabet!

What goes up if the rain comes down?
An umbrella!

What has one horn and lots of milk?
A milk truck!

Why did the boy put candy under his pillow?

So he could have sweet dreams!

What starts with gas but only has 3 letters?

A car!

What goes up and then down but doesn't actually move?

Stairs!

What fruit do vampires eat?
Necktarines!

What do birds send out at night?
Tweets!

What has one head, four legs but only one foot?
A Bed!

Why are pirates pirates?
Because they ARRRRRRRRRR!!

What stays in the corner and but then
travels all over the country?
A stamp!

What does every winner lose in a race?
Their breath!

What did the big cow say to the small cow?
Mooooooove over!

What kind of key will never unlock a door?
A monkey!

Why did the boy take his ruler to bed?
To see how long he slept!

Funny Tongue Twisters!

Tongue Twisters are great fun!
Start off slow.
How fast can you go?

Sharp smart shark.
Sharp smart shark.
Sharp smart shark.

Frog flip frog.
Frog flip frog.
Frog flip frog.

Three tree twigs.
Three tree twigs.
Three tree twigs.

Baboon bamboo.
Baboon bamboo.
Baboon bamboo.

Frogs feet flash.
Frogs feet flash.
Frogs feet flash.

Six sly shrimps.
Six sly shrimps.
Six sly shrimps.

Watching washing.
Watching washing.
Watching washing.

Fried fish fresh.
Fried fish fresh.
Fried fish fresh.

Five flying frogs.
Five flying frogs.
Five flying frogs.

Black back bat.
Black back bat.
Black back bat.

Chip shop chips.
Chip shop chips.
Chip shop chips.

Bubble blower.
Bubble blower.
Bubble blower.

Cheap ship trip.
Cheap ship trip.
Cheap ship trip.

Swim swam swum.
Swim swam swum.
Swim swam swum.

Sneaker speakers.
Sneaker speakers.
Sneaker speakers.

Sixish sixish sixish.
Sixish sixish sixish.
Sixish sixish sixish.

Three free trees.
Three free trees.
Three free trees.

Free fleas flew.
Free fleas flew.
Free fleas flew.

Six thick sticks.
Six thick sticks.
Six thick sticks.

Fresh fish fly.
Fresh fish fly.
Fresh fish fly.

Six slow snails.
Six slow snails.
Six slow snails.

Big black bug.
Big black bug.
Big black bug.

Gum glue grew.
Gum glue grew.
Gum glue grew.

Bonus Funny Jokes!

Why do bees hum?
They don't know the words!

What did the sheep eat for a snack?
A baaaa-nana!

Where do baby pigs live?
In their playpen!

Why did the cat jump on the computer?
To catch the mouse!

What is the wettest animal?
A rain-deer!

What song does Tarzan love at Christmas?
Jungle Bells!

What kind of dog can tell the time?
A watch dog!

Which type of fish swims at night?
A starfish!

How did the pig write a letter?
With his pig pen!

What did the dad potato name his son?
Chip!

Where do fish sleep?
In their river bed!

What do you give a lemon that has hurt itself?
Lemon-aid!

Why was it so hot at the football game?
Most of the fans had left!

Why did the chicken join the band?
She had the drumsticks!

What sound does a train eating make?
Chew chew!

Why did the snake cross the road?
To get to the other ssssssside!

Why was the tiger in trouble?
He was always Lion!

What do you call a very rich elf?
Welfy!

Which fruit is no fun?
A grizzly pear!

Where do pirates buy their food?
At the Marrrrket!

What did the cloud wear under his coat?
Thunderpants!

Why did the cow eat all your grass?
It was a lawn moo-er!

How do small bees get to bee school?
On the school buzz!

What did the elephant wear in the pool?
Swimming trunks!

What is the best time to go on a trampoline?
Springtime!

How do snowmen get to work?
On their icicle!

Why do golfers wear 3 pairs of pants?
In case they get a hole in one!

Where do cows go on their day off?
The Mooseum!

What do you call a fairy who hasn't had a bath?
Stinker Bell!

Why did the fish live in salt water?
Pepper made her sneeze!

Which day do fish hate?
Fryday!

What is the best day to go to the pool?
Sun-day!

What do you call a dog with a sore throat?
A husky!

How did the fish get to work?
He hailed a crab!

Why did the toilet paper roll down the hill?
To get to the bottom!

Where did the car go for a swim?
The carpool!

Bonus
Knock Knock Jokes!

Knock knock.

Who's there?

Sofa.

Sofa who?

Sofa these jokes have been funny!

Knock knock.

Who's there?

Nanna.

Nanna who?

Nanna your business! It's top secret!

Knock knock.

Who's there?

Hippo.

Hippo who?

Hippo birthday to you! Hippo birthday to you!

Knock knock.

Who's there?

Amma.

Amma who?

Amma not going to tell you until you open this door!

Knock knock.

Who's there?

Sawyer.

Sawyer who?

Sawyer lights on so I thought I would knock!

Knock knock.

Who's there?

Snow.

Snow who?

Snow business like show business!

Knock knock.

Who's there?

Who Who.

Who Who Who?

How long have you had a pet owl?

Knock knock.

Who's there?

Stew.

Stew who?

Stew early to go home! Let's go to the park!

Knock knock.

Who's there?

Duncan.

Duncan who?

Duncan doughnuts go really well with ice cream!

Knock knock.

Who's there?

Buster.

Buster who?

I'm catching the Buster school tomorrow. How about you?

Knock knock.

Who's there?

Owl.

Owl who?

Owl be very happy when you finally open the door!

Knock knock.

Who's there?

Anita.

Anita who?

Anita new key for this door!

Knock knock.

Who's there?

Wendy.

Wendy who?

Wendy doorbell works, please let me know!

Knock knock.

Who's there?

House.

House who?

House it going my oldest friend?

Knock knock.

Who's there?

Red.

Red who?

Red quite a few jokes today so let's read a few more!

Knock knock.

Who's there?

A Tish.

A Tish who?

I think you need to see a doctor!

Knock knock.

Who's there?

Lava.

Lava who?

I Lava you so much!

Knock knock.

Who's there?

Izzy.

Izzy who?

Izzy doorbell working yet?

It's been 3 years!

Knock knock.

Who's there?

Les.

Les who?

Les go to the beach while it's still sunny!

Knock knock.

Who's there?

Nun.

Nun who?

Nun of your business my good sir!

Knock knock.

Who's there?

Jethro.

Jethro who?

Jethro a rope out the window and I'll climb up!

Knock knock.

Who's there?

Lion.

Lion who?

Lion down because I'm really tired! Goodnight!

Knock knock.

Who's there?

Candy.

Candy who?

Candy door be answered faster next time please?

Knock knock.

Who's there?

Ben.

Ben who?

Ben knocking so long I forgot why I'm here!

Thank you so much

For reading our book.

I hope you have enjoyed these funny jokes for 5 year old kids as much as my kids and I did as we were putting this book together.

We really had a lot of fun and laughter creating and compiling this book and we really appreciate you for reading our book.

If you could possibly let us know what you thought of our book by way of a review we would really appreciate it 😊

To see all our latest books or leave a review just go to
kidsjokebooks.com
Once again, thanks so much for reading.

All the best,
Jimmy Jones
And also Ella & Alex (the kids)
And even Obi (the dog – he's very cute!)

Made in the USA
Las Vegas, NV
10 February 2023

67286080R00066